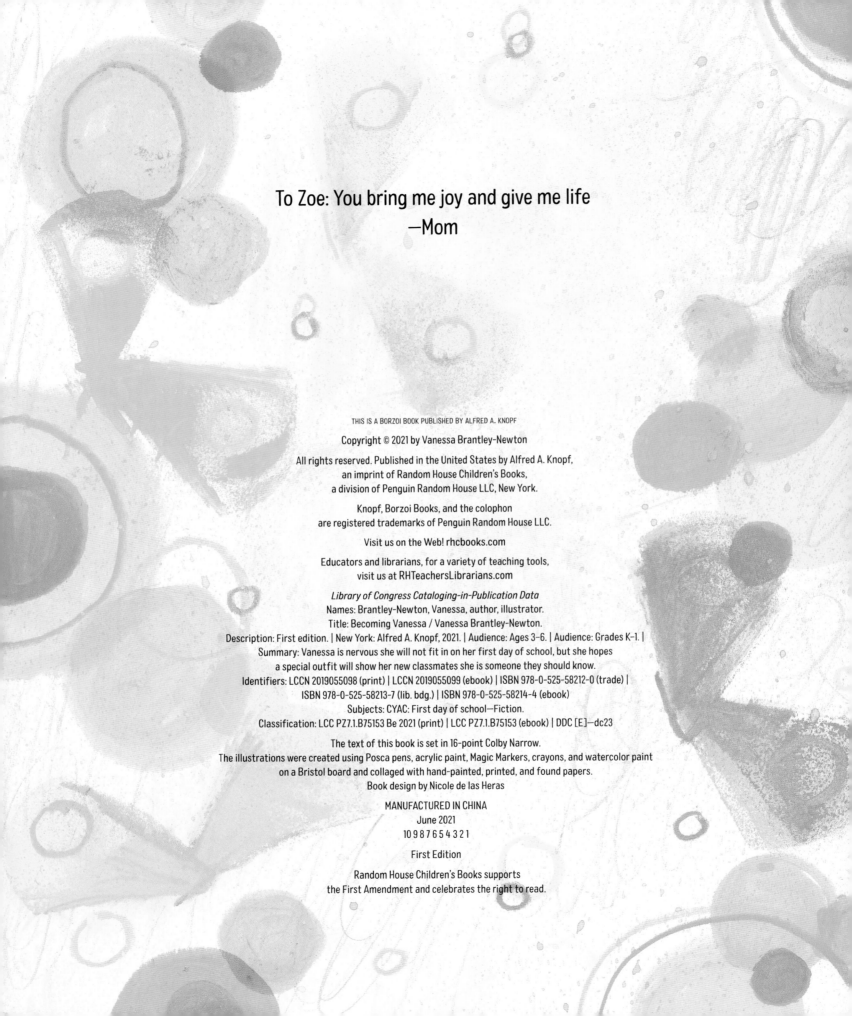

To Zoe: You bring me joy and give me life
—Mom

THIS IS A BORZOI BOOK PUBLISHED BY ALFRED A. KNOPF

Copyright © 2021 by Vanessa Brantley-Newton

All rights reserved. Published in the United States by Alfred A. Knopf,
an imprint of Random House Children's Books,
a division of Penguin Random House LLC, New York.

Knopf, Borzoi Books, and the colophon
are registered trademarks of Penguin Random House LLC.

Visit us on the Web! rhcbooks.com

Educators and librarians, for a variety of teaching tools,
visit us at RHTeachersLibrarians.com

Library of Congress Cataloging-in-Publication Data
Names: Brantley-Newton, Vanessa, author, illustrator.
Title: Becoming Vanessa / Vanessa Brantley-Newton.
Description: First edition. | New York: Alfred A. Knopf, 2021. | Audience: Ages 3–6. | Audience: Grades K–1. |
Summary: Vanessa is nervous she will not fit in on her first day of school, but she hopes
a special outfit will show her new classmates she is someone they should know.
Identifiers: LCCN 2019055098 (print) | LCCN 2019055099 (ebook) | ISBN 978-0-525-58212-0 (trade) |
ISBN 978-0-525-58213-7 (lib. bdg.) | ISBN 978-0-525-58214-4 (ebook)
Subjects: CYAC: First day of school—Fiction.
Classification: LCC PZ7.1.B75153 Be 2021 (print) | LCC PZ7.1.B75153 (ebook) | DDC [E]—dc23

The text of this book is set in 16-point Colby Narrow.
The illustrations were created using Posca pens, acrylic paint, Magic Markers, crayons, and watercolor paint
on a Bristol board and collaged with hand-painted, printed, and found papers.
Book design by Nicole de las Heras

MANUFACTURED IN CHINA
June 2021
10 9 8 7 6 5 4 3 2 1

First Edition

BECMING
VANESSA

Vanessa Brantley-Newton

Alfred A. Knopf
New York

Mom pulled at Vanessa's hair as she got it ready for the first day of school. Mom was excited, and Vanessa could tell she wanted her to be excited, too. Vanessa wasn't so sure. "What if the other kids don't like me?"

Over breakfast, Dad told Vanessa not to worry. "I know you're nervous now, but you'll come home bursting with stories to tell us. I can't wait to hear all about your new classroom, and teacher, and friends. How could they not like a special girl like you?"

Kiddos

"But how will they *know* I'm special?"

Mom and Vanessa decided she should pick out her own first-day-of-school outfit so her new classmates could tell right away that she was someone they should know.

Vanessa chose each item of clothing carefully.

Her tutu.

A feather boa.

Her polka-dot leggings and shiny new shoes. And her favorite hat.

By the time she got her jacket and new backpack on, she felt ready.

Dad walked her to school.

Miss Delaney did seem nice. But the other kids didn't get
Vanessa's outfit in the way she'd hoped they would.

While everyone got settled, Vanessa met some of her classmates.

"Hi! I'm Megan, and this is Bella. We live on the same street."

"I'm Liam."

"I'm Todd!"

"My name is Vanessa."

Then it was circle time, where everyone would introduce themselves.
"Vanessa, look at your outfit! Why don't you go first?" said Miss Delaney.
"My name is Vanessa. I like to draw. My favorite thing to draw is
butterflies. I'm going to be a big sister soon."

"Thank you, Vanessa! Does anyone have any questions for our new friend?"

"'Vanessa'? I've never heard that name before!"

"Why are your shoes so shiny?"

"You dropped a feather."

Next, everyone wrote their name. Vanessa noticed it took a lot longer for her than anyone else.

When she looked at Megan's neatly printed letters, Vanessa had an idea to make her day a little easier.

"Can anyone tell us what animal this is?" Miss Delaney asked.

Megan raised her hand. Vanessa did, too.

"Megan?"

"It's a caterpillar!" Vanessa shouted.

"Vanessa, I called on Megan."

"My name is Megan now, too."

"No, it's not! Your name is *Vanessa*."

After that, things only got worse.

"I can't see
past her hat!"

"Too many feathers!"

Even her shoes were pinching her feet.

This day wasn't special. Her outfit wasn't special.
And neither was Vanessa.

School
BUTTERFLY
GARDEN

When Vanessa got home, she didn't want to tell Mom and Dad about her day. She didn't want to talk at all.

She wrapped herself up in her blankets, pushing her classroom and her very un-special day as far away as she could.

In the morning, she picked out a different outfit.

"Are you sure that's what you want to wear? Don't you want to add a special accessory?" Mom asked.

"I don't want to be special today. I don't want to be Vanessa. I just want to be left alone."

"You don't want to be Vanessa? Why would you say that?"

"Vanessa is long and hard to write! Why couldn't you have named me Megan or Bella? They don't even have to write any *s*'s—and I have to write two!"

"Do you know why I named you Vanessa? Vanessa means 'metamorphosis'—that's what a caterpillar does when it turns into a chrysalis and comes out a butterfly. I gave you a name that would help you become whoever you want to be. You're my butterfly."

"So, are you ready to go back to school?"

"Almost."

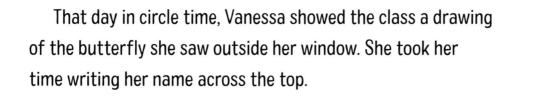

That day in circle time, Vanessa showed the class a drawing of the butterfly she saw outside her window. She took her time writing her name across the top.

She didn't need her boa or her new shoes for them to see she had something special to share.

"I saw a butterfly, and that is what my name means."

"Vanessa means 'butterfly.'"